The AMAZING DAYS of ABBY HAYES

What Goes Up
Must Come Down

Read more books about me!

The AMAZING DAYS of ABBY HAYES

What Goes Up
Must Come Down

ANNE MAZER

LITTLE APPLE

SCHOLASTIC INC.
New York Toronto London Auckland Sydney
Mexico City New Delhi Hong Kong Buenos Aires

ISBN-13: 978-0-439-82926-7
ISBN-10: 0-439-82926-7

Text copyright © 2008 by Anne Mazer.
Illustrations copyright © 2008 by Scholastic Inc.
All rights reserved. Published by Scholastic Inc.

SCHOLASTIC, APPLE PAPERBACKS, THE AMAZING DAYS OF ABBY HAYES, and associated logos are trademarks and/or registered trademarks of Scholastic Inc.

12 11 10 9 8 7 6 5 4 3 2   8 9 10 11 12 13/0

Printed in the U.S.A.   40

First printing, April 2008

For more information about Anne Mazer
please visit www.amazingmazer.com

To the wonderful students at Norwood Public School in New Jersey.
Thanks for a great visit! I loved the questions!

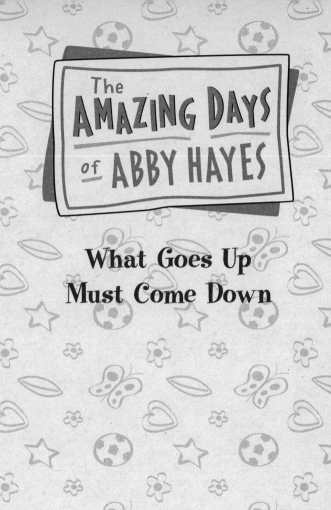

The AMAZING DAYS of ABBY HAYES

What Goes Up
Must Come Down

Chapter 1

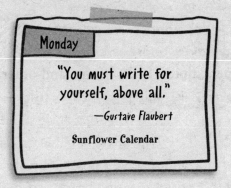

Monday

"You must write for
yourself, above all."

—Gustave Flaubert

Sunflower Calendar

That's what I usually do. I write for
myself every single day. No one reads my
journal but me.

But now something has changed.

I'm going to write for a lot of people:
everyone I know, and their friends, parents,
siblings, cousins, and neighbors.

I'm going to write for the entire city!

No, I'm not going to publish my journal.

No, I'm not going to post online.

No, I'm not going to write on public bill-
boards.

I bet you're curious now. Well, you'll have to wait, because I have to announce something equally or even more exciting:

(Trumpets, flutes, bells, horns, and other music)

My family is going to Paris this week.

Trip Timeline:

1. My mother receives invitation to speak at a legal conference in Paris, France.

2. She accepts.

3. My father decides to look for cheap tickets on the Internet.

4. He finds them. The whole family will go to Paris with our mother, even though it's not a school vacation.

5. Strangely enough, at first, three members of the Hayes family do not want to go to Paris.

(Question: Are we crazy? Answer: Probably.)

6. We don't want to miss literary journal meetings, debate society, athletic practices, dances, parties, etc.

7. Dad persuades us. Paris is one of the most fascinating cities in the world. This is a once-in-a-lifetime trip.

8. Fourteen-year-old Isabel realizes how much history is in Paris.

9. Her athletic twin, Eva, says that she'll walk all over Paris. Paris is a good city for walking, she says.

(ANY city is a good city for walking and jogging, if you ask Eva.)

10 Nine-year-old Alex doesn't need persuading. He's thrilled to get out of school.

11. I'm <u>still</u> not sure about this trip, so I talk to my favorite teacher, Ms. Bean.

"You don't want to go to Paris?" Ms. Bean gasps when I tell her. "Well, you can stay here and teach my class. Do you think your family will adopt me?"

She's kidding, right?

I wonder: If Ms. Bean joins our family, will she fight my older sisters for her morning cereal?

Will she argue over who got the most awards in ninth grade?

And will she call herself Ms. Bean-Hayes? Or Ms. Hayes-Bean? "Paris," Ms. Bean sighs, interrupting my fascinating thoughts.

"Think of the art, Abby!" she says. "All the world-class museums: the Louvre, the Musée d'Orsay, the Orangerie, the Cluny, the Centre Georges Pompidou, the Rodin Museum..."

"Um, yeah." My head starts to spin.

"Paris has some of the world's greatest architecture," Ms. Bean continues. "Its history goes back to before the Roman Empire."

"Really?"

"The city is known for its art, politics, science, music, fashion, and food, to name just a few." Ms. Bean is really excited about my trip. "And, Abby, I know you'll love Paris. Writers from all over the world have lived there."

My eyes light up.

"The city is famous for writers," Ms. Bean repeats.

Suddenly I can't wait. "Will I meet any?"

Ms. Bean suddenly grabs the newspaper, folds it back, and hands it to me. "Look!"

I don't understand. Then, I see it.

The newspaper is running a special series called "Journeys: Ordinary People Writing Extraordinary Stories."

This week's story features a trip to China.

Ms. Bean says, "They've never used a student writer for this series and I think it's about time. You'd be perfect."

"Me?" I squeak.

Ms. Bean whips out a cell phone and begins to dial.

"Is this the features editor?" she asks. "I have a talented sixth-grade writer here. She's going to Paris with her family. She'd like to write something fabulous for your 'Journeys' series. Are you interested?"

It's as simple as that.

My article must be five hundred words or less. Photo is optional. Deadline: a week after my return.

I'm now a foreign correspondent for the local newspaper.

<u>Food for Thought:</u>

I will be the first student, <u>ever</u>, to publish in "Journeys."

If I do a good job, I'll open the door for other students to do the same.

If I don't, I won't.

My audience will be the entire city.

When they read my article, people might

not know my age. They might even think
I'm an adult, like everyone else who writes
for "Journeys."

I'll have to write as well as a grown-up.

How would a grown-up write?

First, they'd have lots of facts about
Paris at their fingertips. (I don't have any!)

Second, they'd go to fascinating, famous
places.

Third, they'd be serious. They wouldn't
write anything goofy.

It's lucky that I'm headed to one of the
most amazing cities in the world. Paris has
inspired some of the world's greatest writers,
artists, musicians, and thinkers.

So why not ME?

Chapter 2

Thursday

"Good things come to
those who wait."

The Promises Calendar

Oh, yeah? The Hayes family already has
good things coming to us. Like Paris, France.
We are on our way!

HOORAY!

That's the good news.
The bad news: Since five a.m. this morning, we have done nothing but wait.
(We have a LOT of good things coming
to us!)

<u>How have we waited?</u>
<u>Let me count the ways:</u>

1. Waited for the taxi to take us to the airport.

2. Waited in a long line to check our baggage and get our boarding passes.

3. Waited in <u>another</u> long line for airport security.

Actually, we are still waiting in line to go through airport security.

Will the waiting ever end? I want to be in Paris already!

Abby shut her journal and slipped it in her jacket pocket. "We've been in this line forever," she complained.

"We're almost at the head of the line," her sister Eva said reassuringly.

"No, we aren't." Eva's twin, Isabel, was always ready to contradict her. "We have at least another twenty minutes."

Abby groaned.

"Shut up, Isabel," Eva said. "You're making it worse."

"*You* shut up," Isabel retorted.

Abby took a step back. She could feel a fight ready to burst out. And they'd only been waiting in line a few hours.

How will I get through this trip? she thought in dismay.

Paris was a once-in-a-lifetime experience — and her family was quite another.

Somehow she had forgotten to mention her family to Ms. Bean. Would she be able to write her article in the midst of all the bickering?

"All right, cut it out," their father, Paul Hayes, said. "If you keep fighting, they won't let you on the plane."

"If the airline knows what's good for it," Abby mumbled under her breath.

As the twins continued to argue, Olivia Hayes shook her head. "Why did I think this trip would be different?"

"But, Mom," Alex said. "Eva and Isabel are always fighting about *something*."

"We aren't always fighting!" Isabel said.

"Are too!" Eva insisted.

"They'll stop by the time we get to Paris," their mother said. But she didn't look like she believed it.

"I'm tired of standing in line. I want to be in Paris already," Alex whined.

"Come on, everybody, lighten up," Paul Hayes said. "This is supposed to be our dream trip."

Dream trip? Abby thought. They hadn't even passed through security yet and already everyone was arguing.

They were going to the City of Lights. She hoped it wouldn't turn into the City of Fights.

She hoped she would survive the dream trip with her real family.

"Listen, all," Olivia Hayes said. "As we go through security, no smart remarks, no arguments with each other or the guards, and don't even *think* about being funny."

She gave her husband a look. "That means you, too, Paul."

"My lips are zipped," her husband said.

Abby craned her neck to see ahead. People were removing their shoes and jackets.

"We have to take off our sneakers?" Alex complained.

"I told you before we left," their mother said. "Weren't you listening?"

Abby wrinkled her nose, thinking of smelly feet. Not a romantic start to the trip. She definitely wouldn't include it in her article.

"Step up, ma'am," the guard said to their mother.

They had finally reached the security checkpoint.

Olivia Hayes slipped off her shoes. Then she placed them with her sweater and purse in a plastic bin.

"Follow my lead," she said to her family.

One by one, they took off their sneakers and put them in plastic bins. They slipped off jackets and sweaters.

They emptied pockets into another bin. Backpacks, carry-ons, and laptops went on the conveyor belt.

"Put that down, miss," a security guard said, pointing to the notebook that Abby clutched under her arm.

"It's my *journal*!" Abby cried in alarm. Nothing and nobody came between her and her journal.

"Don't worry, they won't eat it," Eva said. "They're just making sure that it's not a weapon."

Abby watched as the conveyor belt carried away her beloved journal.

"I've *never* used my journal as a weapon," she said.

"Once in a while I want to throw it at one of my sisters, but I never do."

"Ha, ha, very funny," Isabel said. "But we're not supposed to joke." She plopped her bag down.

The security guard rifled through its contents.

He pulled out a supersize bottle of nail polish. "You can't take this on the plane," he said. "No liquids over three ounces."

"But . . ." Isabel began to protest.

"Sorry," the guard said.

"I can't live without nail polish!" Isabel cried.

"Never mind, Isabel," Paul Hayes interrupted. "There will be plenty of nail polish in Paris."

Eva smirked. "Why paint chemicals on your nails, anyway? It's not good for you, or the environment, or for airline travel. . . ."

"Shut up," Isabel said. She elbowed her sister.

"I'm so sorry," their mother said to the guard with an apologetic smile. "They're not usually like this."

"They're worse," Abby muttered under her breath as she followed her sisters through the metal detector.

Another security guard waved a wand over her.

"You're all clear," the guard said. She smiled at the Hayes family. "Have a good trip."

"Thank you," Olivia said.

Abby grabbed her journal. She slipped on her shoes and shouldered her backpack.

The family headed for the departure gate.

Their trip to Paris had officially begun.

Chapter 3

Thursday

"Be like a postage stamp;
stick to one thing until
you get there."

—Josh Billings

The Glue-Stick Calendar

I'm stuck to one chair in the airport lounge. Will that get me to Paris?

Question That <u>No One Will Answer:</u>
Why did we get to the airport two hours early when the plane was going to be two hours late?

Mom says these things happen when you're traveling.
Dad says be glad that we're not having a snowstorm or other extreme weather event.

People have sometimes gotten stuck in an airport lounge for days.

I don't want to even think about that!

Being in the airport lounge for hours is bad enough.

The Airport Lounge:

Hard plastic seats.

Noisy.

Crowded.

Uncomfortable.

Nothing to do but wait . . .

And wait some more.

Those Who Wait:

Alex: sleeps with mouth open.

Occasionally wakes up to play hand-held game.

Isabel: checks nails obsessively. Will she chip one before we get to Paris? A possible tragedy when no nail polish in her bag.

Eva: jogs around lounge. Almost knocks over innocent, unsuspecting bystanders.

Mom: works on laptop. Doesn't notice anything.

Dad: pretends to read magazine. But really eating all the candy we brought for the airplane.

Me: writing, of course. Taking notes for article? I don't think I want to write about THIS.

I want to write about famous monuments, famous people, and famous places.

I want to write about what it's like to be in Paris. Will I feel like a different person?

I hope so.

Airport lounges are the most boring places on earth.

People Who Wait With Us:
Man talking loudly on cell phone.
Woman knitting long, striped scarf.
Sailor chatting with white-haired lady.
Woman reading medical magazine.

I am watching the knitting lady as her scarf gets longer and longer and longer and longer. . . .

Note: This plane better show up soon! Otherwise she will knit a scarf long enough to reach Paris!

One-and-one-half hours later: It's time to board the plane. FINALLY!

Five minutes later: Boarding is just another Waiting Opportunity.

Twenty-five minutes later: I am older and wiser, and not yet on the plane.
Why did I think that boarding was going to be easy? That I'd just walk on and take my seat?

How to Get On a Plane:
(Hint: V-E-R-Y S-L-O-W-L-Y)
1. Wait for your boarding zone to get called.
2. Stand in line of people with same zone.
3. Show your passport and boarding pass to a uniformed person.
4. Walk down a long, cold tunnel with lots of people in a hurry.

5. On the plane! Hooray!

6. Can't move forward. Stuck in small, cramped aisle.

7. Must wait for person in front of you to stuff huge, bulging bag into tiny overhead compartment.

8. Sit down in seat next to nice knitting lady. Hooray!

9. In wrong seat. Stewardess asks you to move.

10. Check your ticket to find correct seat.

11. It is between Isabel and Eva Hayes.

12. They aren't speaking to each other.

13. Have a _fabulous_ trip!!

Cheering or Crying? Your Vote, Please . . .

1. We're finally on our way!

2. I'm seated between my sisters until we get to Paris.

(Is this like being between a rock and a hard place? If yes, which sister is which? And what do I do?)

Plane Math:

I am stuck in one place for seven hours with two sullen sisters and zero room to move.

The stewardess just served us five pretzels in a foil pack and half a glass of soda.

I have one set of earphones to listen to three CDs.

Summary: The airline lounge added up to a miserable few hours. But it now equals paradise.

Chapter 4

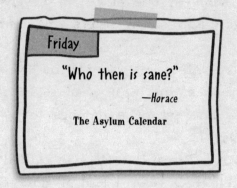

Not <u>my</u> family!

We got to Paris late last night. I was too tired to cheer. We checked into the hotel and went up to our rooms.

My sisters and I have a view of the rooftops of Paris. Mom and Dad's room looks down into a courtyard garden.

I have my very own, very tiny hotel room. It connects to my sisters' room. (But they can't come in unless I let them!)

The bed is tucked under the eaves, next

to a small window. It has a purple quilt on it. My favorite color!

If I had been less tired, I would have been TOTALLY inspired! I would have started my newspaper article right then and there.

But it felt like we had been traveling for weeks. All I wanted to do was to climb into bed and go to sleep.

I was pulling on my purple polka-dotted pajamas when I heard a knock on my door.

"Who is it?"

"Isabel. Want to come out for a walk?"

"_No!_"

"Don't you want to breathe the Parisian air?"

"I can breathe it in my room," I said.

"Come on, Abby! Where's your spirit of adventure? Eva's coming, too."

"She's crazy," I said. "And so are you."

"Okay, be that way. But everyone's going, including Mom and Dad and Alex."

"Everyone? Why didn't you say so in the first place?"

I didn't want to be in a strange hotel, in a strange city, without my family nearby. Even if they WERE insane.

I pulled on my jeans and threw a sweater on over my pajama top. Hopefully, no one would notice the purple polka dots.

"Wait!" I yelled. "I'm coming with you."

Report from Paris, France
By your reporter, Abby Hayes

At midnight, the insane Hayes family, fresh off a long, exhausting Transatlantic trip, set off for a pleasant little stroll around the darkened streets of Paris.

Correction: It wasn't pleasant or little. It wasn't a stroll, either.

It was a long and tiring walk.

We interrupt this report for a brief rant.

WHAT'S THE MATTER WITH MY FAMILY? I'M EXCITED TO BE HERE, TOO, BUT I DON'T HAVE TO TRAMP AROUND THE STREETS OF PARIS AT MIDNIGHT. EVEN ALEX THOUGHT IT WAS FUN.

WHAT WERE THEY THINKING?
ARE THEY INSANE?
WHY? WHY? WHY?

We walked until we reached the Seine
River.

There my family held the following conversation:

Actual Hayes Family Conversation —
I Am Not Kidding!

"It's the Seine!"
"It's the Seine!"
"It's the Seine!"
"It's the Seine!" (rhymes with "oh, no, not
again")
"It's the Seine!" (rhymes with "when" will
they stop saying that)
"It's the Seine!" (rhymes with "I better
count to ten")
I think you get the idea.
Then the conversation took an unex-
pected turn.
"Look, it's a boat!"

"A boat? Is that a boat?" (um, DUH!!!!)
"Yes, it's a boat!" (Help me, <u>please</u>.)

Was this jet lag? Or something worse?
Just when I thought that everyone had lost their mind for good, they all stopped talking.
It was like someone waved a wand. We were all silent, as if under a spell.
Lights sparkled on the water. The bridge was mysterious and beautiful. A boat drifted silently past.
My tiredness disappeared.
Suddenly, it was all worth it.

Her hair still wet from the shower, Abby slid into an empty chair in the hotel café.

She placed her journal on the table and unfolded a napkin. "Anything good to eat here?"

Her father pointed to a basket filled with pastries. "Straight from a Parisian bakery."

"You mean *boulangerie*," Isabel corrected.

"Boo-what?" Alex asked.

"It's French for 'bakery,'" Isabel lectured. "We should all learn at least a dozen new French words."

"What's French for 'Shut up'?" Eva asked sweetly.

"Won't you please wait until I've finished my espresso before you begin your morning fight?" their father begged.

Abby plunked a croissant on her plate. A waiter poured steaming hot chocolate into her cup.

"Thank you," Abby said. "I mean, *merci.*"

"Very good, Abby," Isabel said in her best schoolteacher manner. "That's *très bien* in French."

"Tray beans?" Eva said.

Isabel groaned.

Abby exchanged a quick glance with Alex. "I bet you two argued in your sleep last night."

"Too tired," Eva said. "As soon as my head hit the pillow, I was out."

"Me, too," Isabel agreed.

Alex took a chocolate brioche from the basket. "What's French for 'handheld games'?" he asked.

"I don't know." Isabel took a napkin and wiped chocolate from his face. "Do you, Eva?"

"Of course not." Eva snatched the last croissant from the basket, destroying the fragile peace.

"*Idiot!*" Isabel cried, with a French accent.

"Stupid!" Eva said, without a French accent.

"Come on, kids," their mother said absent-mindedly. She was studying some notes for her conference. "We're in Paris."

"Well, *duh*!" Isabel said.

Paris or no, it was breakfast as usual for the Hayes family. No one mentioned the midnight walk by the Seine.

Abby took a sip of the hot chocolate. It was thick, rich, and dark.

Her father smiled at her. "Not bad, huh?"

"It's delicious," Abby said.

"Where's the pool?" Eva suddenly asked.

"You mean, *la piscine*," Isabel corrected.

"There's no pool in this hotel," Paul Hayes said.

"But we *always* have a pool!"

"And cable TV," Alex added. "I want to watch cartoons."

"I don't have a hair dryer in my room, either," Isabel said. "Isn't Paris supposed to be about luxury and pampering?"

Olivia Hayes looked up from her papers. "This hotel *is* a bit bare-bones," she agreed.

"Where's everyone's sense of adventure?" Paul Hayes asked. "This is a terrific hotel, chock-full of charm."

"And not much else," Isabel complained. "I thought you were going to book us into someplace good, Dad."

Paul Hayes shrugged. "I booked at the last minute. I didn't have a lot of choice. We were lucky to find this hotel."

"My room has a great view of the rooftops of Paris," Abby spoke up. "I might write about it in my article. It's so . . . French."

She pictured nibbling on croissants in a Parisian café as she searched for the perfect word.

Maybe someone would ask her what she was doing. And she would tell him or her that she was working on a newspaper article.

"I'm going to describe the rooftops," she whispered to herself.

That is, if rooftops weren't too ordinary. Abby didn't want to waste her four or five hundred words on something unimportant.

"This hotel may be French, but that's about all you can say for it," Eva was saying.

Abby couldn't understand her family. Last night they were raving about the Seine River. This morning they were complaining about the hotel.

How could they be so contradictory?

And how could they prefer cable TV to genuine Parisian atmosphere?

Olivia Hayes sighed. "Do we really want to waste our time on this? The hotel isn't ideal, but it's decent."

"The beds are comfortable, the showers are hot. . . ." Paul Hayes said.

"And breakfast is good," Alex added with his mouth full.

"I love this hotel," Abby said. "I love my sloping roof and the sink in the corner. I even love my tiny room."

"*You* would," Isabel said.

"What does that mean?" Abby demanded.

"Girls, girls." Paul Hayes sighed. "Enough arguing. We have an exciting day of sightseeing ahead of us."

"I can't wait," Eva said. "We'll probably spend all our time fighting about what to do."

"You're right about that," Abby said.

"I want to go off on my own," Isabel suddenly said. "I mean, with Eva. We're old enough."

"All right," her father said.

Isabel gasped. She obviously hadn't expected him to agree. "Mom? Is he serious? Can we really go off on our own?"

"If you and Eva promise to stay together," her mother answered. "And take a map, your cell phones, and plenty of money."

"*Awesome*," Eva breathed.

Abby stared at them enviously. Roaming Paris on their own — she wished that she was old enough to join them. But there was no chance that her sisters would want *her* tagging along.

Would she really want to be with them, anyway? Since the family had pulled out of the garage early yesterday morning, her sisters hadn't stopped arguing.

"We'll visit Notre Dame, the Arc de Triomphe, and the Eiffel Tower," Eva rattled off.

Abby groaned in envy. It sounded like a dream day.

"I have some other ideas," Isabel began. "What about . . ."

"Alex and I were talking about Parisian parks and gardens," her father interrupted before the twins began to argue again. "Then we'll hit the science museum. . . ."

"*Yeah!*" Alex said.

"How does that sound to you, Abby?" her father asked.

"That's it?" Abby didn't hide the disappointment

in her voice. "Some parks and gardens? And a science museum?"

She didn't think she'd get inspiration for her article from some trees or shrubs. Even if they *were* growing in Paris.

As for the science museum, there were plenty of those at home. That wasn't something that she'd choose to write about, either.

"You can decide tomorrow, Abby," her father promised.

"Or you can come with *us* today," Isabel offered.

Now it was Abby's turn to gasp. Or maybe she hadn't heard right. Had Isabel just invited her to join them?

"Only if you want to," Isabel said. "Would you rather spend the day with Dad and Alex?"

"*No!*" Even if Abby's sisters drove her crazy most of the time, she'd still drop everything for a chance to tour Paris with them. If they really wanted her, that was . . .

"You're inviting me for real?"

Isabel shrugged. "Sure. Why not?"

"Of course, silly!" Eva said. "We'll have a girls' tour."

Abby turned to her parents. "Can I?"

Her father looked at Isabel and Eva. "Will you all stick together? Can you get along for a day? Will you watch out for your younger sister?"

"Yes," Eva and Isabel said in unison.

Abby threw her arms around her older sisters. What a story she'd have for the newspaper!

Three sisters on their own in Paris. Maybe Eva and Isabel would even help her with ideas.

"You're the greatest!" she cried.

Chapter 5

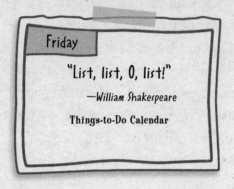

Friday

"List, list, O, list!"

—William Shakespeare

Things-to-Do Calendar

Isabel, Eva, and I couldn't agree on what to do today, so we have each made a list.

Isabel's list

My oldest sister is happy seeing <u>anything</u> old. But there are so many ancient things in Paris that it's hard to narrow it down:

1. Visit ancient Roman baths
2. Visit place where Marie Antoinette was imprisoned
3. Visit historic city hall
4. Visit historic Montmartre cemetery

Eva's list

Eva wishes she could run in the Paris marathon, but it's the wrong time. We also missed the Tour de France and three soccer matches.

1. Jog over the bridges of Paris

2. Jog under the Arc de Triomphe

3. Jog around the Eiffel Tower

4. Jog to Notre Dame

Abby's list

A lot of what I know about Paris comes from picture books. Like <u>Madeline</u>. Will I see Miss Clavel on the streets?

The rest of what I know comes from Ms. Bean. It would be great to write about the famous writers who lived in Paris.

1. Visit homes of famous writers
2. Visit writers' cafés
3. Visit statues of famous writers
4. Visit places that inspired writers

<u>New and strange reason to make lists:</u>
To find things NOT to do.

Since we didn't agree on anything, we decided to find something that no one wanted to do.

I mean, we wanted to find something to do that wasn't on our lists. In other words, we agreed to disagree so we can agree.

If you understand <u>that</u>, you win a free French baguette with butter and chocolate.

Yes, a chocolate and bread sandwich. And it's delicious! It just shows how much we can learn from other cultures.

Eva, Isabel, and I plan to visit at least one French bakery today.

Oh, and I almost forgot!

We finally decided to go to the Louvre. It's practically the greatest museum in the world. I'm going to see the <u>Mona Lisa</u>!

Seeing the <u>Mona Lisa</u> will be PERFECT for my article. It can't get more inspiring than that!! I'm going to have SO much to write about!

I can't wait!

The Hayes family gathered in the hotel lobby.

Olivia Hayes, dressed in an elegant pale blue silk suit and high heels, had just left for her conference.

The rest of the family members were more casually dressed in jeans and T-shirts. Each had a backpack or a travel bag. Paul Hayes wore sturdy sneakers. So did Alex, Eva, and Abby.

Only Isabel wore pointy-toed green leather shoes.

"Are you *sure* you can walk in those things?" her father asked her.

"Dad! This is Paris!" Isabel sniffed. She had somehow made her T-shirt and jeans look especially elegant today, with scarves, a belt, and jewelry. "I refuse to wear ugly shoes in Paris."

Eva rolled her eyes.

"Besides, they're *very* comfortable," Isabel said.

"If you say so," her father said. He didn't look convinced. "If I were you, I'd pack a pair of sneakers in that bag."

"Not necessary," Isabel insisted.

"Don't say I didn't warn you. Is everyone ready to go?"

Eva checked her inner pockets. "Passport, credit cards, guidebook, cell phone," she recited. "And subway card."

"I've got the same," Isabel said. She took a lipstick out of her purse and began to touch up her lips.

"Abby?" her father asked.

"I have extra money, a subway map, and the address of the hotel written on a piece of paper," Abby said. "And my journal, water, and snacks."

"You'll check in regularly, like we agreed," their father reminded them for the hundredth time.

"We'll be fine," Eva said impatiently. She knelt down to tighten her sneaker laces. "Isabel and I aren't going to fight. We're going to look after Abby. We'll all stick together. Don't worry about us."

"Maybe I should worry about the Parisians instead?" her father asked. "Or the tourists at the Louvre?"

"I can't wait to see all the famous paintings!" Abby cried.

"We must see ancient art at the Louvre," Isabel said. She began to count off on her fingers: "Egyptian, Assyrian, Greek, and Roman . . ."

"What about French art?" Eva asked.

"Don't forget the *Mona Lisa*," Abby said.

For a moment, the three sisters glared at each other. Then they all burst out laughing.

"See, Dad? We can get along," Eva said.

"Let's go," their father said. He held open the front door of the hotel.

The family walked out into the street.

"The City of Lights," Isabel said in a dazed voice. "There's so much to see and experience. . . ."

"Watch your step," Eva said, grabbing her sister's arm. "You almost stepped in dog poop."

"Ewwww," Abby said. Another thing *not* to write about.

"Missed it!" Isabel said triumphantly.

Their father looked at Isabel's pointy green leather shoes and sighed. Then he pointed down the street. "There's the entrance to the Metro."

The Metro was the Parisian subway.

"Good-bye, Dad! See you later!"

"Have a great day!" Paul Hayes called out to his daughters. "Stay together! Look both ways before you cross the street!"

Isabel, Eva, and Abby let out a collective sigh. Then they descended into the Paris Metro.

They were on their own.

Abby held on to a strap in the subway car and let the unfamiliar sounds of the French language wash over her.

From time to time, she glanced at her two older sisters. They looked as awed as she felt.

"Can you believe we're here on our own?" Isabel said. "We're in Paris! Doesn't everyone look stylish?"

"I wish I had taken French instead of Spanish in school," Eva said. "Then I'd be able to understand what people are saying."

"I've been studying French for a couple of years," Isabel admitted, "and I can only catch a few words."

"What if we need to ask for directions?" Abby asked. "Or find a bathroom? Do we use sign language? Or draw a picture?"

"Don't worry, I'll see you through," Isabel reassured her.

Abby sighed. Sometimes her sisters were annoying, but right now they were the absolute best.

"Here's our station!" Eva cried.

It seemed as if the ride had taken no time at all. The subway squealed to a stop. The doors opened and everyone rushed out of the train.

Abby halted on the platform to stare. She had never seen a subway station that looked like a museum.

Marble sculptures were set into the walls behind.

glass. They looked like the real thing. But they couldn't be, could they?

Without thinking, Abby reached for her journal. She wanted to sit down on a bench and start writing immediately.

"It's just a subway station, silly," Isabel said. But she sounded awed, too.

"Oh," Abby said. "I knew that."

Eva squeezed her hand. "If the subway station is like this, can you imagine the museum itself?"

The three sisters mounted the stairs. They emerged blinking into the light.

Chapter 6

Friday

"Fear, desire, hope still push
us on toward the future."

—Michel de Montaigne

Romantic Illusion Calendar

<u>My desire:</u>

To actually get inside the Louvre.

<u>My hope:</u>

To soon be in front of the <u>Mona
Lisa</u>.

<u>My fear:</u>

That Eva, Isabel, and I will stand in
the admissions line for another few hours!
We have been here forever: a whole hour
and a half!

Will fear, desire, and hope push us on toward our future? Or will we be stuck in this line outside the museum for the rest of the day?

At least there are plenty of things to look at . . .

1. The Louvre itself.
2. An awesome glass pyramid.
3. Tourists from all over the world.

We just met an Australian family.

They say "cuppa" for cup of tea and "lolly" for sweets.

They call little kids "ankle biters."

I can't wait to tell my best friend, Hannah! I'll say something like, "Let's have a cuppa and some lollies, and don't let the ankle biter near us!"

The Australian family made us smile. They made our long wait bearable.

Good news:

We are finally inside the Louvre. (Only had to stand in line for two hours and seventeen minutes.)

Bad news:

There are two billion other people in the museum.

Where did they all come from? The streets of Paris must be completely deserted!

It's so crowded here that we can barely move.

Isabel, Eva, and I are trying to hold on to each other.

We're being pushed in every direction.

Eva just yelled, "If we get separated, let's meet in the lobby in an hour."

Good news:

It's good she said that because . . .

Bad news:

We just lost each other.

I can't see my sisters!

The crowd is pushing me forward.

I don't know where they're taking me.

Good news:

We're heading for the Mona Lisa.

Bad news:

I can't see anything; there are too many people surrounding it.

Good news:

Just caught a glimpse of <u>Mona Lisa</u>'s chin!

Bad news:

Lost it!

More bad news:

I am being pushed out of the room by the crowd.

Good news:

I see an uncrowded gallery.

It's a room with gigantic ancient stone sculptures.

Isabel is here!

I am really relieved to see her.

More good news:

She knows where Eva is.

Bad news:

We were going to find Eva, but we got lost again.

Good news:

We wandered through some interesting rooms.

We saw the medieval Louvre.

We saw the Greek, Etruscan, and Roman rooms.

And the Egyptians . . .

And we walked through Napoleonic rooms dripping with gold, velvet, and crystal chandeliers.

Bad news:

While searching for Eva, Isabel and I looked at so many portraits and coins and furniture and sculptures and painted ceilings and different periods of history that they are all jumbled together in our heads. . . .

And we both have headaches.

Is this my dream day in Paris?

<u>Good news:</u>

We ran into Eva on one of the staircases.
We're all together again!

<u>Good news yet again:</u>

Everyone has had enough of museums.

We're going to sit down and have some lunch. Then we might wander over to the Luxembourg Gardens.

Maybe we'll meet Dad and Alex there?

Chapter 7

Cake?

Why eat cake?

In Paris there are also
strawberry, kiwi, and peach
tarts, eclairs, babas, meringue puffs, chocolate mousse, and cream puffs.

After lunch, Eva, Isabel, and I bought
a box of pastries from a French patisserie.

We took them to the Luxembourg Gardens.
We're going to sit on a bench and eat just
a few. We'll save the rest for Dad, Mom,
and Alex.

"My stomach hurts." Eva let out a small moan. She leaned back on the park bench and closed her eyes.

Isabel slipped her feet out of her pointy leather shoes and wiggled her toes. "My stomach *and* my feet hurt."

Abby felt sick, too. "I don't think I'll ever eat again," she groaned.

"Me, neither," Isabel agreed.

The pastries had been so delicious that the three sisters had gotten carried away. They had kept on eating "just one more" until the box was empty.

Abby glanced at the crumpled box next to them on the bench. "We should have saved just a few," she said. "The rest of the family will be so disappointed."

"They won't know," Eva said. Her eyes were still shut. "I'm not telling."

Isabel rubbed her reddened toes. "I'm too stuffed to move," she said. "And I'm too sore to walk. How will we get back to the hotel?"

"We won't," Eva said.

"We'll camp on this bench tonight," Abby said. "Or else they'll have to airlift us out of here."

"I wouldn't mind staying in the Luxembourg Gardens for a few days," Isabel said, gazing at the trees. "It's so peaceful here."

"But not on a bench!" Eva said. "Even our pathetic hotel is better."

"It's not pathetic," Abby protested weakly. But her stomach hurt too much to argue.

Still, she felt strangely content.

The Hayes sisters were getting along nicely together. They had stuck together, helped each other out, and hadn't fought at all, unless you counted a few minor sisterly disagreements. And those had been mostly friendly.

It wasn't the awe-inspiring Parisian day Abby had hoped to experience for her article, but it was still not a bad one. . . .

Abby tossed a few leftover crumbs to some pigeons on the sidewalk. They clustered around her feet, begging for more.

"Sorry, we pigged out," she told the pigeons.

She opened her journal, stared at the last entry she had written, and shut it.

"Nothing to write about today?" Isabel asked.

"My head is whirling," Abby complained. "It's

crammed with the sights and sounds and tastes of Paris. I can't think, much less write."

"Are you getting a few ideas for the newspaper article?" Eva asked.

"Not exactly," Abby admitted.

"They probably don't include getting lost in the Louvre and gorging on pastries," Isabel said.

"You're right about that," Abby said.

Isabel glanced at her watch. "We have to meet Dad and Alex at the hotel in an hour," she said. "I vote for taking a taxi."

"It's just as easy and a lot cheaper to take the Metro," Eva countered.

"Whatever," Abby said, bracing herself for an argument. But everyone was too tired to pursue even a minor disagreement.

"Okay," Isabel said to Eva. "You're right."

That had to be one for the *Hayes Book of World Records*.

Abby put away her journal. Then she stumbled over to a garbage can to throw out the pastry box.

Eva zipped up her backpack. Her face looked pale.

With a deep groan, Isabel slipped her feet back into her pointy shoes.

The three sisters limped toward the Metro.

This wasn't how it was supposed to be, Abby thought, loosening a button on her jeans. Paris was supposed to be romantic, thrilling, and unusual.

All she wanted now was to get to the hotel before she was sick to her stomach.

As Eva, Isabel, and Abby stumbled through the front door of the hotel, Alex practically flew over to meet them.

"We saw an exhibit on aliens! We went to a plan-etarium!" he cried.

"Isn't that nice," Isabel said wearily. She slipped off her shoes and headed for the stairs to her room.

"Why don't we have an elevator?" she wondered out loud.

"It's authentic," her father said.

"So are my sore feet." Isabel sagged against the banister.

Her father shook his head, but didn't say anything.

"We went into a submarine, too," Alex said to Eva.

"Later, Alex." Eva sounded almost more tired than Isabel. She followed her twin to the stairs.

"And we saw some really cool volcano stuff." Alex tried to get a response from Abby next.

"Um, that's very fascinating, Alex." Abby rubbed her eyes. Her stomach didn't hurt so much anymore, but she felt like lying down on the floor and sleeping for a few months.

"We had a terrific day," her father said. He and Alex didn't look tired at all. In fact, they looked ready to go out sightseeing again.

But they probably hadn't visited the most crowded museum in the world, walked across the Seine to the Luxembourg Gardens, and eaten an entire box of rich pastries by themselves.

"Did you have a good time?" her father asked Abby.

"It was great, Dad," Abby said, trying to keep her eyes open. She swayed on her feet. "I'm going upstairs . . . to lie down. . . ."

Their father shook his head. "I've never seen you three so worn out. You must have had some day."

"Um, yeah," Abby said. She began to drag herself up the stairs.

The last thing she heard was her father calling after her.

"Have a nap, a hot shower, and get dressed in your best clothes," her father called.

"No, no!" Eva cried.

Isabel only groaned.

"We're going out tonight," Paul Hayes announced, "to a real French bistro."

Chapter 8

It is VERY wearisome to hear people complaining!

Just ask Mom and Dad and Alex.

They had to put up with me, Isabel, and Eva. We complained all the way to the bistro last night.

<u>Hayes Family Mood-o-Meter</u>
<u>(on leaving for bistro):</u>

Mom: In happy mood. Had presented paper at conference that morning. A great success. Everyone loved it.

Dad: Also in happy mood. About to eat fine food at fine bistro in Paris with fine family.

Alex: Ecstatically happy mood. Chattering about alien communication nonstop.

Isabel: In very cranky mood. No appetite and blistered feet. Forced to don sneakers for elegant dinner in Paris. Let everyone know exactly how miserable she was.

Eva: Thought of food made her feel ill. Took it out on the rest of the family.

Abby: Head spinning. Eyes closing. Wished everyone would just shut up.

Hayes Family Mood-o-Meter
(on arriving at bistro):

Mom: Cranky. Exasperated and aggravated by grumpy daughters.

Dad: Cranky. No longer looking forward to delicious meal.

Isabel: Extremely cranky. Hot teenage boy saw her sneakers and snickered.

Eva: Utterly cranky.

Abby: Stupendously cranky.

Alex: Oblivious. Still talking about aliens. If he can ignore cranky family, he must BE an alien!

Hayes Family Mood-o-Meter (inside bistro):

In spite of our extremely bad moods, we all cheered up a bit on walking into the bistro.

Le Bistro:

1. The tables were set with rose-colored tablecloths.

2. There were low lights on paneled walls and a patterned carpet.

3. Everyone around us was speaking French.

4. It almost felt like we had walked onto a French movie set. IT WAS AWESOME!

5. Then we had to wait a long time for the waiter. (This wasn't too bad, because there were a lot of fascinating people to stare at.)

6. French waiters aren't perky. Our waiter didn't say, "Hi, I'm Jacques, your server for this evening."

7. Confession: I actually don't know what he said, since it was in French. But it didn't <u>sound</u> perky.

8. Using our rusty French, our family managed to order food. Although we weren't sure exactly what we ordered.

9. Then we waited for a very long time again. When the food came, Isabel, Eva, and I were finally getting hungry.

10. The waiter poured wine into Eva's and Isabel's glasses!!! (But Mom and Dad didn't let them drink it.)

11. Interesting fact: Do you know that in France, they have cheese at the end of a meal? They serve a selection of cheeses instead of dessert.

12. Unpleasant fact #1: Some cheeses smell like old feet.

13. Unpleasant fact #2: Some cheeses taste like old feet!

I forgot to mention that the food was delicious! (Except for a few of the cheeses.)

By the end of the meal, no one was cranky any more.

We walked back to our hotel slowly late at night. I thought about including the bistro in my article.

But even though we had a wonderful evening, I don't think it was special enough. I mean, it was just a meal.

Maybe today I'll have the perfect Parisian moment?

Chapter 9

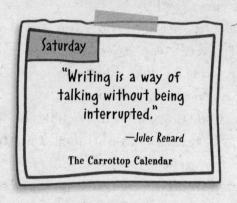

Did he know my family?

Writing is the ONLY way I can talk and not be interrupted.

After spending so much time on vacation with my family, I have just one thing to say: Thank goodness for my journal!

Writing in my journal is like taking a deep breath of air in a crowded room.

The empty pages are so peaceful. They never argue, contradict, lecture, advise, interrupt, or refuse to listen.

They give me time to think and clear my head.

I'm SO glad that I have a few minutes to write this morning before we go out sight-seeing again.

Being around my family 24/7 is kind of intense – even though my sisters have had a complete personality change since we arrived in Paris. They are (mostly) acting as if they actually like me!

They are (mostly) treating me like a real person!

I hope they don't change back to their old selves when we get home again.

I have some more good news.

Perfect Parisian Privileges:

Eva, Isabel, and I can go out on our own again!!!

HOORAY!

Dad and Mom declared that the "experiment" was a success. (That's because we didn't tell them about the pastries.)

They said that we had proved that we could get along together, stay safe, and have a good time.

They even gave us each extra money to spend.

We have another whole day in Paris ahead of us!

The world is our oyster!

NOTE: That's what Dad said. It makes no sense at all. Why would we want the world to be an oyster?

I'd rather have it be my peach!

Or my ice cream cone!

Or my gigantic bowl of popcorn!

(Yes; I REALLY have my appetite back.)

Today's Goals:

1. See Paris. HOORAY!!!
2. Shop for souvenirs.
3. Get along with sisters.
4. Don't gorge on French pastries.
5. Walk everywhere.
6. Figure out what I'm going to write about.

Three loud knocks sounded on Abby's hotel room door.

"Who is it?" Abby asked.

"Eva and Isabel!"

"Just a minute!" Abby laced up her sneakers and stuck a flowered wallet in her backpack. Then she skipped over to the door and unlocked it.

At the sight of her two sisters, Abby's mouth dropped open.

Isabel, the fashionista, was dressed in a long skirt and a ruffled blouse. Her nails were newly painted and she wore makeup, as usual.

But she had traded her pointy-toed green leather shoes for comfortable sneakers.

That wasn't like her at all. Even with blisters, fashion came first for Isabel.

Eva, the athlete, was wearing a long lime green T-shirt and sporty pants. But she had actually put on lipstick and painted her nails.

That wasn't like *her*, either. Eva never wore makeup or nail polish. It was practically a badge of honor.

Seeing Abby's stare, she grimaced. "It's Paris," she said.

Isabel gave her sneakers a sad glance. "I've

got bandages on three of my toes," she sighed. "I had no choice — unless I wanted to lie in my room all day."

"Well, I'm ready." Abby hadn't made any concessions to fashion or pain. She was wearing her usual outfit of jeans, a striped T-shirt, and a hoodie.

She picked up her backpack and locked the hotel door behind her.

As the three of them galloped down the stairs to the hotel lobby, Isabel made an announcement. "Eva and I have a plan."

"What is it?" Abby said, a little nervously.

"How about this: We each get to choose an activity for the day. Then we do all three. Isn't that brilliant?"

Isabel paused on the landing. She perched a wide-brimmed hat on her head. "Does this look cute or stupid?"

"Cute," Abby said.

"Stupid," Eva said at the same time.

Isabel scowled at both of them.

"So I get to choose, too?" Abby asked. That was the important part.

"Of course, silly." Isabel glanced at her reflection in a window. "But you ought to know that

Eva and I want to visit the Île St. Louis and the Île de la Cité."

"Eels?" Abby repeated. "Where are the eels in Paris?"

"*Eel*," Isabel pronounced. "An *île* is an island. The Île St. Louis has seventeenth-century houses and a village atmosphere. It's a very special part of the city."

She continued as if she were reading from a guidebook. "The Île de la Cité is the oldest part of Paris. There we will discover the Cathedral of Notre Dame."

"A cathedral? We're going to *church*?" Abby said in disbelief. "Why? It's not even Sunday."

"Notre Dame is a Gothic masterpiece," Isabel said primly. "It's almost a thousand years old."

"If we have time, we'll visit the prison where Marie Antoinette waited to be beheaded," Eva said, as if she were promising a treat.

Abby shuddered. "No, thanks."

"And don't forget the Seine," Eva said. "We're going to talk a long walk along the *quais*."

"But we already did that," Abby protested.

Eva smiled mysteriously. "We have a surprise or two up our sleeves."

"Oh, boy," Abby mumbled. She knew all about

Eva and Isabel's surprises. She didn't want any part of them. Especially if they had to do with prison cells or churches.

If you asked her, the day didn't sound too promising. She wondered if she was ever going to find that "perfect Parisian moment" to write about.

But, even if she didn't, spending the day with Eva and Isabel was undoubtedly better than spending it with Dad and Alex.

At least, she hoped so.

"What do *you* want to do, Abby?" Isabel asked. "You haven't told us yet."

"Me?" She had almost forgotten that she had a right to choose one third of the day. Abby took a breath.

"Today I want to be inspired," she announced. "I want to go to a writers' café. And see where famous writers lived."

That would be a subject worth writing about.

"Paris is known for its international community of writers," Isabel said in a schoolteacher's voice.

"Maybe we'll meet one?" Abby said hopefully.

Eva jogged over to the lobby door and swung it open for her two sisters. "Maybe it's you," she said.

"Me?" Abby repeated. "I haven't even started my article yet. All I do is write in my journal."

"Doesn't that count?" Isabel asked.

"No," Abby said. "Real writers write books and articles. And this one has to be extra-special."

Chapter 10

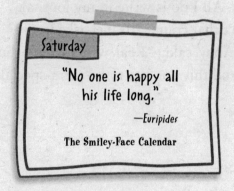

Saturday

"No one is happy all
his life long."

—Euripides

The Smiley-Face Calendar

Happy a whole <u>life</u> long?

I just want to be happy for a week! Or even for a few hours today.

Our day at the Louvre wasn't a very happy day.

It was a day of crowds, confusion, and constant noise.

It was a day of seeing too many gold-encrusted clocks, too much walking, and way too many pastries.

It was a day when Isabel, Eva, and I felt overwhelmed, overtired, and overfed.

We finally relaxed at the bistro, though. And I felt happy being with my family.

I don't expect to be extremely happy today. I have to do a lot of things that Eva and Isabel want to do.

My activity will only take a couple of hours. Still, we ARE going to a writers' café! I'm so excited!

That will be my moment of happiness for today.

And maybe my happiness will last even longer when I turn it into the subject of my article!

Bad News Bulletin:

Isabel has just pointed out a few problems with my wonderful plan:

1. When we visit the writers' café, how will we recognize the writers? Will they wear signs around their necks stating: "Writer here!"

2. If they do, the signs will be in French. . . .

3. The writers will, of course, also be

speaking French, or maybe even other foreign languages. . . .

4. Therefore, I will not understand a word of what they're saying.

5. Even if I do, will I be brave enough to speak up and introduce myself?

6. And, finally, as Isabel also pointed out, famous writers' cafés are the last place to find writers.

The cafes are filled with tourists like us. Real writers will be home writing.

Conclusion: We are not going to a writers' café. Why bother?

Another conclusion: Why does Isabel have to be so logical? It spoils all the fun!

Still another conclusion: Is this just another way for Eva and Isabel to do everything THEY want? And to talk me out of what I want?

Final conclusion: I no longer have a good idea for my article! Why does it keep on eluding me?

(Note: "elude" means "escape." As in

"The meaning of the word 'elude' does not elude me.")

To cheer me up, Eva says that we can all visit a famous ice cream shop on the Île St. Louis.

(Note: Every time one of my sisters says <u>île</u>, I can't help thinking of eels. Are we going to have octopus ice cream? Or eel sherbet? I'd like to see my sisters eat a lobster ice cream sundae. With crayfish on top!)

The promise of ice cream doesn't make me feel better.

Ice cream can't take the place of a writers' café. Even really great ice cream.

And I'm definitely not going to write an article about eating ice cream on some Parisian island.

Isabel just announced that we are crossing the Pont Neuf on foot.

<u>Fact</u>: Pont Neuf means "new bridge." The new bridge is actually the oldest bridge in Paris.

Another fact: Isabel has been up all night reading guidebooks.

And something else: Both Eva and Isabel are excited about visiting Notre Dame and the Eels.

They think it'll be a great focus for my article. They have been trying to persuade me for the last half hour.

I know they're trying to help, but I wish they would leave me alone!

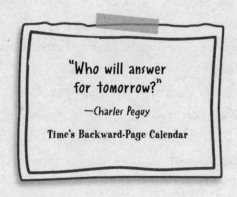

"Who will answer
for tomorrow?"

—Charles Peguy

Time's Backward-Page Calendar

ME. I will answer for tomorrow.

Since my sisters talked me out of the one and only thing I wanted to do, I'M going be in charge of tomorrow.

And they better not argue about it, either!

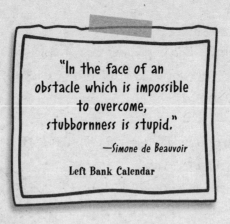

"In the face of an
obstacle which is impossible
to overcome,
stubbornness is stupid."

—Simone de Beauvoir

Left Bank Calendar

No comment.

And now, I will draw a curtain over the next part of the day, which means I close my journal and follow my sisters to their precious Eels in a suspicious, sullen, sinister silence. . . .

Six hours later:

"Life is a great surprise."
—Vladimir Nabokov

Butterfly Calendar

Um, yes it is.

I'm glad that pages can't blush.
Because this one would be furiously blush-
ing right now.

A Surprise: Isabel, Eva, and I had a
FANTASTIC day.

Another Surprise: I loved
the Eels. (Or the Îles!)
I loved Notre Dame. We
walked in on a concert.
The musicians were play-
ing on very old instruments. I
pretended that I was living in the Middle
Ages. (It worked until someone's cell phone
beeped.)

Notre Dame was built before trains, fac-
tories, engines, machines, and cars were
invented. It was built before computers, the
Internet, television, handheld games, cell
phones, and DVD players. They didn't even
have movies!

The Surprises Keep Piling Up: The Île St.
Louis was really cool, too.

More Surprises: I loved the ice cream!

<u>Another You-Know-What</u>: We saw medieval buildings! And old Roman baths!

<u>Can You Stand Another One</u>? We saw where Marie Antoinette was in prison. It was creepy but fascinating.

<u>An Excellent Surprise</u>: Eva led us to two huge markets. One market was all birds; the other was all flowers.

<u>Best Surprise of All</u>: The walk along the Seine. The sidewalk is lined with secondhand booksellers. They are called <u>bouquinistes</u>. (Never mind how to pronounce it; I have no idea.) I bought an old map of Paris.

I'm definitely going to put this in my article!

Hooray! We had the BEST day in Paris together! Even though I didn't get to do what I wanted, I still loved it.

<u>Strangest Surprise</u>: When I got back to my room, I sat down to write my newspaper article. I felt totally inspired. At last!!

But I couldn't write a word.

Not a single one.

Chapter 11

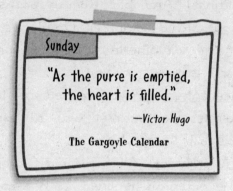

That's what's happening to us!

Isabel, Eva, and I have emptied our purses to buy pastries, ice cream, crepes, and other delicious Parisian treats.

We have emptied our purses for museum admissions, souvenirs, scarves, makeup, books, maps, toys, and other fun things.

We spent <u>all</u> the money that our parents gave us, plus our allowances and birthday money.

But as we empty our purses, our hearts fill with new thoughts and experiences. Yesterday was the BEST day!

And today is going to be even better.

Hooray, hooray! Our hearts are still full, and now our purses are full again, too!

Mom and Dad gave us extra cash. They didn't even lecture us about spending too much money.

THANK YOU, MOM AND DAD!!!!

Isabel, Eva, and I have decided to do something extra-special today. We're going to visit the Eiffel Tower. . . .

It's over a thousand feet high. Usually I'm afraid of heights, but this is Paris.

I'm going up, no matter what!

"Look! There it is!" Isabel cried, pointing to the Eiffel Tower as they exited the Metro.

Abby gazed up.

It was one thing to think about climbing the Eiffel Tower in the safety of her hotel room. It was another to actually stand in front of it. The Eiffel Tower looked like a monster Tinker Toy. It dwarfed the entire city.

Abby suddenly felt sick. "We're going to the top of *that*?"

"Isn't it awesome?" Eva was practically jumping for joy. "You can see all of Paris from the top. I can't wait!"

"It has a post office and a restaurant, too." Isabel played the guide, as usual. "Abby, I want you to take a picture of me sipping an espresso on top of the Eiffel Tower."

"Um, yeah, sure, I guess," Abby stammered. She kept looking at the tower.

"It has stood here for over a hundred years," Isabel continued. "Over two hundred million people have visited it."

"You can walk up to the second level," Eva added. "It's good exercise and a lot cheaper. Then you take an elevator to the top."

Abby couldn't suppress a small groan.

"What's the matter?" Isabel asked. "Aren't you feeling well?"

"It's so, um, tall." Abby's face felt hot. "And so, uh, big."

"Of course it is! That's the point!" Eva said. "We'll have a bird's-eye view of the city."

"I'd rather have the worm's-eye view," Abby mumbled.

"Come on, Abby, where's your sense of adventure?" Isabel asked.

"Don't worry, the Eiffel Tower is very safe," Eva reassured her. "Thousands of people go up every day. No one gets hurt."

Abby shook her head. "I'm sorry," she said. "I just can't."

She wished she could toss her fears away. She wished she didn't have to spoil Eva and Isabel's day. She wished she could join in on a Parisian adventure that was tailor-made for her article.

But she knew she couldn't handle it. She felt dizzy and nauseous just *thinking* about going up the Eiffel Tower.

Eva and Isabel exchanged glances.

"Maybe you and I can go up one at a time," Isabel suggested to Eva. "The other one of us will stay with Abby."

"That would take *hours*," Eva said. "There's a

long line for the elevator to the top. Even if we're all together, it's going to take quite a while."

"You two can go up," Abby offered. "I don't mind waiting."

Isabel shook her head. "We have to stay together."

"And anyway, how can we enjoy ourselves when you're all alone here?" Eva said.

Abby pointed to a park bench a short distance away. "I can sit on that bench and take notes for my article," she said. "I'll be perfectly happy. And I promise I won't go anywhere. Even to the bathroom."

Her sisters looked at each other again.

"I have my cell phone, money, the hotel address, and my Metro ticket," Abby said. "Really, I'll be fine."

"It's not a good idea," Isabel said.

"Nothing can go wrong," Abby persisted.

Eva looked thoughtful. "It would only be an hour or so."

"Do you really think it's okay?" Isabel asked.

"You two go enjoy yourselves," Abby said firmly. "I'll be writing in my journal right there on the bench. Don't worry about me."

* * *

Abby sat on the bench, feeling very grown-up as she wrote in her journal. Her sisters had trusted her to stay on her own.

She would show them how independent and trustworthy she was.

Crowds of people swirled around her. Tourists sat down nearby, people chatted on cell phones, kids bought snacks from the vendors lining the walk.

She kept on writing. Abby covered pages with descriptions of the city and the people she saw. She still didn't have a clear idea for her article, but at least she was taking notes.

Ms. Bunder, her fifth-grade writing teacher, always said to get *everything* down on paper.

The sun was much higher now. Her sisters were taking a long time, but they had warned her that might happen. They must have gotten stuck in a line somewhere.

Abby didn't envy them. She was happy on the bench, watching all the people and writing in her journal.

She felt almost like a real writer, sitting there on her own.

"Excuse me, but are you American?" A young, college-age woman sat down next to Abby.

Abby closed her journal and smiled up at her. "Yes, I am. But how did you know?"

"I noticed you writing in English," the young woman said. "And I made a lucky guess. Sorry to interrupt, but you remind me so much of my younger sister."

"I *am* a younger sister," Abby said.

"Well, I'm an American college student. I'm living with a French family and I'm desperately homesick." The young woman stuck out a hand. "My name is Clara."

"I'm Abby." She moved over on the bench to make more room for her. Clara looked somehow familiar.

"How long have you been in Paris?" Clara asked.

"A few days," Abby said.

Clara sighed. "I've been here for six months. I miss my family and my little sister. I wouldn't even mind being back at Misty Acres."

"Misty Acres?" Abby repeated.

"That's a swanky development where my cousin lives. I hate it there."

"That's weird," Abby said. "My family just moved to a place called Misty Acres."

"Wow," Clara said. "But it can't possibly be the same Misty Acres."

"That's the kind of thing that only happens in books," Abby agreed.

"I lived with my relatives for a couple of months after high school," Clara explained. "It was kind of a lonely place. There was no one my age nearby. I was stuck with my younger cousin."

Abby made a sympathetic noise.

"Brianna's the same age as my sister, but she's nothing like her."

"There's a Brianna who lives in *my* Misty Acres."

She and Clara stared at each other.

"It's a popular name," Clara said slowly. "But it couldn't possibly be the same person. That's too much of a coincidence."

"Yeah," Abby agreed. She wanted to ask if Clara was related to the biggest bragger in sixth grade. But she didn't want to be too blunt. "Is your Brianna, um, a model and an actress? Is she good at, uh, *everything*?"

"That's my Brianna," Clara said. "Better than the best."

"Oh, my gosh, it's got to be her," Abby cried. "Does she act in commercials? Is she related to the mayor?"

Clara sighed deeply. "I think we're talking about the same person."

"I can't believe this!" Abby exclaimed. "We're practically neighbors!"

"That's amazing!" Clara said. Then she frowned. "I've gone back to Misty Acres for the holidays. I ought to know you. Did your family buy one of those new houses under construction?"

Abby nodded. "We moved only a couple of months ago. Misty Acres is a lot fancier than our old neighborhood."

"It's fancier than my neighborhood, too," Clara said. "My family isn't as wealthy as Brianna's. But I prefer our old house on our old street."

"Me, too! I know exactly what you mean!"

Abby and Clara looked at each other.

"What are the chances of something like this happening?" Clara asked. "Probably one in a zillion."

"But it makes a weird kind of sense," Abby said. "Brianna is related to *everyone*."

"Even me," Clara said ruefully.

"She won't believe I met you in Paris."

Clara jumped up. "Would you like to grab a bite to eat?" she asked. "I know a great café."

"I wish I could." Abby was getting hungry. "But I have to wait here for my sisters."

"Maybe they can join us," Clara offered.

"They'd love that." Abby hoped that they wouldn't get upset that she had talked to a stranger.

Though now Clara was more like a neighbor.

In all her dreams of Paris, Abby *never* imagined sitting alone on a bench and striking up a conversation with someone who turned out to be related to Brianna.

This Paris trip was taking the strangest twists and turns.

Chapter 12

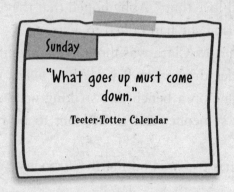

Sunday

"What goes up must come down."

Teeter-Totter Calendar

Eva and Isabel went up in the Eiffel Tower almost three-and-a-half hours ago. They <u>have</u> to come down sometime.

What are they doing up there, anyway?

Is Isabel getting her nails painted in fifty different colors at an Eiffel Tower nail salon?

Is Eva jogging the stairs until she drops?

WHEN are they going to come down?

"This is getting annoying," Abby said, glancing at her watch. "I don't know where my sisters are."

"Maybe they met some cute guys their age," Clara suggested. "Maybe they forgot about the time."

"That's not like them," Abby said doubtfully. "I can't imagine what happened. If you weren't here, I'd be bored to death."

Even Abby couldn't write in her journal for three-and-a-half hours.

She and Clara had been having a great conversation. First, they talked about Brianna, and then they moved on to Misty Acres.

And then, they talked about Paris. Abby told Clara what it was like to tour the city with her sisters, and Clara told her about the French family she lived with, her classes, and what it was like to live in another country.

"It's very good, but I miss my home," Clara concluded. "And I'm starting to dream in French. I hope I remember how to speak English when I go home."

"You're doing fine with me," Abby reassured her.

She looked up, hoping to see Eva and Isabel hurrying toward her. But all she saw was an endless stream of strangers.

It made her feel abandoned and alone. How could her sisters have forgotten about her?

"Don't wait for my slow sisters," she said. "Go to lunch without us."

Clara shook her head. "I don't feel right about leaving you," she said slowly. "I'll stay until your sisters show up."

Abby took a deep breath. She felt suddenly nervous. If Clara didn't want to leave her alone, could that mean that something might be wrong?

"Do your sisters have cell phones?" Clara asked.

"Of course!" Abby cried. "I have one, too. Why didn't I think of it sooner?"

She'd never had a phone before, but her father had gotten them the cell phones for exactly this kind of situation.

Abby reached into her backpack, then looked up with a puzzled frown. "My phone isn't there."

"Don't worry, we can use mine," Clara offered. "Do you have your sisters' cell numbers?"

"I wrote everything down on a slip of paper and put it in my wallet." That was Dad's idea, too. He had insisted that she have backup information.

Abby felt a rush of gratitude toward her father. He had really thought of everything.

But her wallet wasn't in the backpack, either.

And neither were her portable music player, her headphones, and a leather change purse she had bought for her best friend, Hannah.

"It's . . . it's . . ." Abby couldn't finish the sentence. She held open the empty backpack for Clara to see.

"Missing?" Clara said.

Abby nodded.

"Did someone bump into you or jostle you? Were there suspicious people next to you on the bench?"

"I don't think so," Abby said. "But I was busy writing in my journal. I wasn't paying much attention."

Come to think of it, someone *had* sat awfully close to her. And there had been a few small, almost unnoticeable tugs on her backpack.

"Oh, my gosh, someone ripped off my stuff!" she cried.

"I'm so sorry, Abby."

Abby felt close to tears. How could someone do this to her? Who would steal from a kid on a bench? What kind of person was that?

Then she began to worry: How would she get back to the hotel? How would she get in touch with her sisters?

For a long moment, neither she nor Clara said anything.

Then Clara sprang into action. "I'm going to try and find your sisters. Describe them to me."

"They're twins, fourteen years old, but not identical," Abby began. "And they're probably arguing about something."

At least Clara hadn't deserted her. And she was a lot more concerned about Abby than her sisters seemed to be.

Unless something really bad had happened to them, too. . . .

Abby prayed that wasn't the case. But if they were okay, why hadn't they come back for her?

"I have an idea," Clara said. "Give me a sheet of paper from your notebook."

Abby carefully tore out a page and handed it to Clara. Then she handed her the pen.

Clara wrote in large block letters, "ISABEL AND EVA, WHERE ARE YOU? ABBY IS LOOKING FOR YOU."

"Our last name is Hayes," Abby told her.

"HAYES," Clara added. "Now I'm going to walk around the Eiffel Tower," she said. "And let's hope that they see this."

"How long will you be gone?" Without her wallet or cell phone, Abby felt alone and defenseless.

"Maybe fifteen minutes?" Clara scribbled down her own cell phone number and handed it to Abby. "If your sisters appear, call me on their cell phone right away."

She hurried toward the Eiffel Tower, holding up the handwritten sign.

As soon as Clara was out of sight, Abby wrote down the cell phone number both in her journal *and* on her hand.

No pickpocket could steal that!

And then she went through her backpack again.

To her relief, she found her passport safely zipped into an inner pocket. She had a few loose coins and a map with the Metro station near her hotel circled in red.

Abby let out a long breath. Now, even if Clara didn't find Eva and Isabel, she might still find her way back to the hotel.

Except that she had forgotten its name and the street address.

That was also written on a slip of paper in her stolen wallet.

She looked up. Clara was back. She was all by herself.

"I couldn't find your sisters anywhere," she said. "Either there were too many people, or they've already left."

Abby tried to keep her voice from shaking. "What do we do now?"

Chapter 13

Sunday

"Everyone needs help from everyone."

—Berthold Brecht

Good Samaritan Calendar

But do I accept help from everyone?

Clara has offered to take me to her apartment. She says the French family she lives with will help me find my family.

Most of my valuables are missing. My sisters have vanished. I don't know how to get back to my hotel. Clara is the only person I know.

But when I think about it, she's really a stranger.

Should I go to the apartment of a person I met on a bench a couple of hours ago?

I wish I could ask an adult what to do, but there aren't any around. I have to make this decision on my own.

My mother always tells me to trust my instincts. My instincts say that Clara is a good person who will help me.

Clara and I took the Metro to her French home. She doesn't actually live in an apartment with a French family; she has her own room in their building.

She gave me a quick peek! It's really small, but cozy. She has a bunk bed and a white bureau. There are stacks of books and pictures on the wall.

Then we went to the French family's apartment and rang their doorbell.

Jean-Pierre opened the door. His wife, Chantal, was right behind him.

Clara spoke to them in French. She pointed a lot at me and made hand gestures.

Chantal kept looking at me and shaking her head. She smoothed my hair and patted me on the shoulder. "<u>Pauvre petite</u>," she kept saying.

Clara translated. "That means 'poor little one.'"

I didn't feel poor or little. But it was
nice that Chantal sympathized.

When Clara was done explaining, Chantal
and Jean-Pierre sat us down at a table.
They gave us mugs of hot milky coffee
and big sandwiches with lots of ham and
butter.

I feel a little better now.

While we ate, Jean-Pierre and Chantal
got out a Parisian phone book and started
making calls.

They are calling every single hotel near
the circled Metro stop on my map. They are
asking for the Hayes family.

I forgot to mention that Jean-Pierre and
Chantal don't speak any English. I don't
speak any French.

Clara is our translator.

The only French word I know is "merci."
That means "thank you." I've been saying
it a lot.

Jean-Pierre and Chantal smile when I

say "Merci." They say "Je vous en prie,"
which means "you're welcome."

Even though I'm feeling a lot better,
I'm still very worried about my sisters. I
hope they're all right. What are they doing
right now?

Are they still in line for the elevator to
the top of the Eiffel Tower?

Or did they have one of their famous
Super-Sister Fights? Maybe the tourists
enjoyed the show so much that they paid
them hundreds of Euros to do it a few
more times.

Or maybe Eva decided to take a thousand and one pictures from the top of the
Eiffel Tower.

She could do it, too! She just put a two-
gigabyte memory card in her camera.

But Jean-Pierre and Chantal think that
my sisters are probably worried about me! I
wish I could tell them I'm having a real
Parisian adventure.

* * *

We haven't found my family yet. Everyone keeps saying that it's only a matter of time.

But if we don't, can I move into Clara's room?

I could sleep on the top bunk and live with her until we found my family. I'd learn to speak French, drink milky coffee every morning at a neighborhood café, and eat lots of ham sandwiches.

It would be great, if my family knew that I was safe.

Chantal just brought out some dessert for us. It's chocolate mousse. It's delicious, but I can't enjoy it as much as I like.

I keep thinking about my family.

NEWS BULLETIN:

We found the hotel! Jean-Pierre asked for "Monsieur or Madame Hayes" and the operator said "Oui."

Then Dad got on the phone.

Hooray! Hooray! Hooray!

* * *

Since Dad doesn't speak any French, Jean-Pierre quickly gave the phone to Clara. She explained what happened.

Even though the phone was halfway across the room, I could hear my father shouting the good news.

And I heard my family cheer.

Then Clara gave the phone to me. For a moment, I was scared.

Maybe Isabel and Eva had disappeared, too. And would my parents be angry that I had gone off with a stranger? Would they ground me for the rest of the Paris trip?

But my mother and father were so happy that I was safe that they didn't ask those questions.

I couldn't say much, anyway. I kept choking up. <u>Everyone</u> was crying. My mother, my father, and my siblings.

Eva and Isabel were at the hotel, too!

When I heard that, I burst into tears.

Then Chantal and Jean-Pierre started to sniffle.

. . .

When I could speak again, Dad asked me to put Clara on the line. He wanted to make arrangements to get me back to the hotel.

She spoke to Jean-Pierre and Chantal in French, then back to Dad in English, then back to French. . . .

You get the picture.

And they made a plan.

While I was on the phone with Dad, he told me why Eva and Isabel had never showed up.

Apparently, my brilliant, talented, over-achieving, extremely organized, revoltingly responsible, superstar sisters forgot where they left me.

They had some pathetic excuses, like "All the benches looked the same." And "We couldn't figure out the signs."

Ha!!! Or, to put it another way, HA, HA, HA!

Actually, it isn't all that funny.

Isabel and Eva searched all over for

me. They yelled my name again and again. When I didn't answer my phone, they panicked.

Then they called Dad. My father told them to take a taxi back to the hotel immediately.

My whole family met in the hotel lobby. They figured that if I was lost, I'd head there.

They didn't know that my cell phone, money, and information had all been stolen.

Everyone had argued about what to do.

Eva had wanted to call the police, Dad wanted to call the American Embassy, Mom wanted to go back to the Eiffel Tower, Isabel wanted to check all the writers' monuments in Paris, and Alex just wanted to find me.

It was a typical Hayes family moment.

Just when they were all having a meltdown, the phone rang.

And they heard the news that I was safe.

* * *

<u>Now</u> I can enjoy the chocolate mousse. My stomach has magically unknotted.

As soon as I'm done, Clara is going to take me back to the hotel.

I'm glad that Clara and I have a little more time together. I hope that we will see each other again when we're home.

When I get home, I hope Brianna will brag about her cousin Clara in Paris. I will agree with every word she says!

Chapter 14

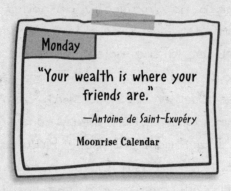

Monday

"Your wealth is where your
friends are."

—Antoine de Saint-Exupéry

Moonrise Calendar

I am wealthier by one friend. Clara is a
solid-gold friend. If it wasn't for her, my
day would have been much, much, much
worse.

Instead, it turned out to be an amazing experience. I got to meet Jean-Pierre
and Chantal and visit an actual Parisian
apartment!

And my adventure wasn't over yet!

On the way home, Clara took me on
a short detour through the market
on Rue Mouffetard. "La Mouff" isn't

world famous like the Eiffel Tower or the Louvre, but I'm so glad I didn't miss it.

It's one of the most ancient streets in Paris. But its market is still alive.

There were street musicians playing at the corners and open stalls of flowers, fruit, and vegetables. There were shining rows of fish on ice and chickens roasting on spits. There were cafés and restaurants, too, and I wished that I could sit in one of the windows and watch for hours.

But we had to get back to my family.

At the hotel, I was immediately surrounded by family members who couldn't wait to hug me.

"Welcome back!" my father said, opening his arms.

My mother couldn't stop hugging and kissing me. "Thank goodness you're okay."

"Did you go to the police station?" Alex asked. "Did you have to speak French?"

Then it was my sisters' turn.

"Sorry we went up the Eiffel Tower without you," Eva whispered. "Don't tell Mom and Dad, okay?"

"Don't they know that already?" I whispered back. "I mean, they know that you couldn't find the bench."

"Mom and Dad weren't very happy that we lost you," Isabel murmured. "We told a little white lie."

"What kind of little white lie?"

"That we left you alone for only five minutes," Eva mumbled.

"You said that?" I squealed.

"We shouldn't have left you for a second," Isabel said, hanging her head.

"But . . ." I was about to say something very stern to my sisters when my mother suddenly noticed Clara standing alone by the door.

"Here's our hero!" she cried and rushed over to hug her.

The rest of the family followed. Then Mom went to get the camera and took snapshots of all of us.

Clara is now six friends wealthier.

She acted like it was no big deal to rescue me. She said that she had been homesick and that I had cheered her up a lot.

When my parents heard that, they immediately invited her to dinner with us. She said yes!

We called Jean-Pierre and Chantal and asked them to join us, too. But they are busy tonight.

Thank you, Clara! Because of you, a bad situation turned into a really good one. But I still wish that some things had been different.

Regrets:

I wish I had paid more attention to the person who sat next to me when I was writing in my journal.

And I wish that I hadn't ignored those little tugs on my backpack.

I also wish that I hadn't lost my wallet, my music, and my cell phone.

I wish that my sisters hadn't gotten in trouble for leaving me alone. I mean, I'm not five years old. I don't have to be watched every second.

But I wish that they hadn't lied, either. Does this force me to lie, too?

I really wish that everyone had known that I was safe all along.

And I wish that my whole family hadn't been so scared for me.

I TOTALLY wish that I had seen my sisters crying over me!

No Regrets:

I'm glad that I didn't lose anything REALLY important, like my passport or my journal.

I'm glad that I'm safe with my family.

I'm glad that Eva and Isabel didn't get in too much trouble. And neither did I.

I'm glad that I met Clara and that she met my family. She was so homesick and now she feels much better.

<u>Unexpected Bonus:</u>

I will be able to blackmail my sisters for the rest of their lives.

A) They lost me in Paris.

B) They couldn't find a bench! How hard is that???

C) My perfect sisters told a white lie!! Yes, those Super-Sib sisters — the ones who lecture me all the time.

Another bonus: They will never be able to lecture me again!!

<u>Even Bigger Bonus:</u>

I think I might have a subject for my newspaper article. "My Amazing Paris Adventure."

YIPPPPPPEEEEEEEEEEEEEEEEE!!!!!!

Abby pressed down on the T-shirts in her suitcase and placed her folded jeans on top of them.

Then she closed her suitcase and, with great difficulty, zipped it up.

"Tight fit," Clara commented.

"There's even more to pack," Abby sighed. "I haven't got everything in yet."

* * *

It was the last day of their Parisian trip. In less than an hour, the Hayes family would be on their way to the airport.

Abby couldn't believe how quickly the trip to Paris had passed. And how much had happened.

Now, too soon, it was time to leave.

She looked in dismay at all the things scattered on the bed.

"Can you leave something behind?" Clara suggested.

"I bought souvenirs for myself," Abby said slowly. "And presents for my friends. I can't leave *those* out."

She went through the list in her mind: a Parisian beret for Hannah to replace the stolen leather purse, watercolors for Sophia, chocolate for Mason, a CD for Natalie, a book of photographs for herself. . . .

"I even got something for Brianna," she confessed.

Clara raised her eyebrows. "Don't you think she has *way* too much stuff already?"

"Well, yes . . . but I saw this totally gorgeous beaded purse," Abby said. "Don't you think that Brianna deserves a present for having a cousin like you?"

"I'm sure she'd agree," Clara said drily. "Though not in the way *you* mean it."

She took a small package from her purse and handed it to Abby. "I hope there's room in your suitcase for one more thing."

"But I should have gotten a present for you!" she cried. "You're the one who did everything for *me*."

"I've had such a great time with you and your family," Clara said. "You took me out to dinner and treated me like one of you."

"You're an honorary Hayes," Abby said. "Though why you'd want to be one, I don't know."

She tore off the wrapping paper. Inside was a journal with a picture of the Eiffel Tower on the cover.

"To remind you of how we met," Clara said.

"I *love* it!" Abby cried. "I'll think of you every time I write in it."

She opened the book.

"It was great to meet you. Keep in touch!" Clara had written her address and e-mail in large letters. And, "We'll meet again in Misty Acres!"

"You have to send me a link to your newspaper article," Clara said.

"I will." Abby hoped that Clara would like what she planned to write about getting lost and finding a new friend in Paris.

There was a knock on the door. Eva poked her head in the room.

"Are you packed yet?" she demanded. "Mom says ten more minutes."

"I'm not even *close* to being done," Abby groaned.

Eva glanced at the piles on the bed. "Just shove everything in your suitcase, Abby. Don't be picky."

With a superior smirk, she slammed the door.

"What do I do now?" Abby cried. "I have too much stuff!"

"Don't worry, we'll figure this out." Clara studied the suitcase. "Look, you can fit some more things in along the edges."

Abby wedged the presents in wherever she could. Then she tried to zip the suitcase shut. The zipper refused to budge.

Clara pushed down on the top of the suitcase, but it still wouldn't close. "What can you leave behind? Your pajamas? An old T-shirt? An extra pair of shoes?"

Abby sighed. Then she reached into the suitcase and took out two pairs of jeans. "You are my Parisian sacrifice," she said to them. "Please don't be offended."

She put them down on a chair.

Clara picked them up. "You don't have to throw them out," she said. "I can mail them to you."

"*Really?*"

"No problem. I should have thought of it sooner."

"You've saved me again," Abby said, with a sigh. "Thank you."

"It's nothing," Clara said. She leaned over to close the suitcase.

This time it closed without a hitch.

Chapter 15

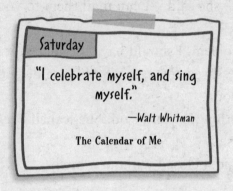

Did Walt Whitman know Brianna?

Isabel tells me he lived during the Civil War. So he couldn't know her.
But who else could he possibly be describing?

Yes, we're home!!! And I just saw Brianna for the first time since we returned from Paris.

Setting:
Tennis courts at Misty Acres, the

fancy new development where my family now lives.

Brianna, of course, has the biggest house of all. It's perched on top of a hill and looks down on all the others.

Main Characters:

Brianna: A vision in pink. Pink miniskirt and pink ruffled blouse. Pink tights. Pink sheepskin boots.

Abby: A vision in grass-stained jeans and holey T-shirt. Holes in ears (no earrings). Old sneakers.

The two of us are sitting in folding chairs by the tennis courts.

Why We Are Sitting in the Setting:

My sister Eva is playing tennis with Brianna's first cousin's mother's aunt's nephew's best friend's girlfriend's boyfriend. Or something.

Actual Brianna Conversation, or ABC of A Bragging Classmate:

WARNING! Please be advised: The

following conversation contains Brianna's best bragging, boasting, self-celebration, and songs of self.

This is not for the faint of heart. Take frequent, cooling sips of chilled water. Do not attempt to read in one sitting.

Start: B looks A over and takes in A's holey outfit. For a moment, she seems unable to speak, then recovers her usual poise.

B: "Interesting" outfit, Abby. Is it for Earth Day?

A: I was working in the garden.

B: My outfit came straight from Hollywood, CA. I bought it at, like, the best boutique.

A: My outfit is straight from the dirty laundry pile.

B (ignores Abby's attempts at humor): Where have you been? Every morning, when my personal chauffeur drives me past the school bus stop, I've looked for you.

A: You mean when your mother drives you?

B: Our limousine has a chauffeur.

A: Oh. Right. Well, I've been on vacation with my family.

B: Camping again?

A: Um, not exactly. We flew to . . .

B (interrupts): We flew to Los Angeles over the weekend and stayed in a four-star hotel. I had, like, a gigantic fruit basket in my room and a box of the best chocolate truffles from . . .

A: My family went to Paris.

B: You mean Paris, Missouri?

A: No.

B: Paris, Tennessee?

A: Not even close.

B: Paris, Kentucky?

A: Um, wrong again.

B (getting frantic): Paris, Texas? Paris, New York? Paris, Illinois?

A: Paris, France.

B (gulps): Oh, that Paris.

A: We visited Notre Dame, the Louvre, the Eiffel Tower. . . .

B: Never mind. We went on a private tour of a movie set and attended a party with, like, dozens of movie stars and drove in a white stretch limousine along Rodeo Drive.

A: Will you be starring in any mov-ies soon?

B: I'm going to be featured in a commercial.

A: Wow! That's awesome! Which one?

B (lowers voice): Um, a donut commercial.

A: A donut commercial? The one where the teenage girl ice-skates with a life-size donut?

B: It's a major role. Thousands of girls tried out for the part.

A: And you'll wear a crown of donuts?

B (stares intently at the tennis courts): I wear a golden Olympic-style skating costume.

A: I suppose donuts are better than bagels.

B: A first-class Hollywood makeup artist does my face.

A: Though it depends whether they're creme donuts, jelly donuts, or sugar donuts.

B (loudly): A top modeling agency has signed me on for more commercials.

Do you know how much money I'm going to earn?

A: Can you eat the donuts afterward?

B: I'll be earning more than our teachers. I'll be so busy that I won't have time to do any homework. But of course I'll still get top grades.

A: Of course. Have you noticed that my sister is beating your first cousin's mother's niece's whatever . . .

B (glares at tennis courts): It must be a mistake.

A: No, I don't think so. . . .

B: He'll triumph, just like all my relatives.

A: Speaking of relatives, I met your cousin Clara in Paris.

B: Oh, her . . . She's not as good as the others. . . .

A: I'm writing my newspaper article about her and how she helped me when I was lost.

B (quickly): Of course you are.

A: Clara is great!

B: She's a member of _my_ family.

A: I almost forgot! I brought you a present from Paris.

B: What? Some tacky souvenir?

A: A very cute purse.

B (waves hand): Oh, don't bother! I already own sixteen Parisian purses in seven different colors. I don't have room in my closet for one more.

A: Are you sure?

B: Thanks, anyway.

There is cheering from the tennis courts. Eva has won.

A: Go, Eva!

B: I demand a rematch!

We will now end the conversation, out of pity for the reader.

WHY did I buy Brianna a present in the first place?

Maybe absence really DOES make the heart grow fonder. When Brianna was far away, I missed her.

Now that she's nearby, I'd like to miss her even more.

* * *

I'm missing Paris, too.

First of all, Clara. It felt like she became a good friend in only a couple of days.

And I miss the delicious pastries, the flower market, the crowds in the Louvre, the subway stops, my tiny room in the hotel, all the people smoking, the hot chocolate, getting lost at the Eiffel Tower, La Mouff, fights with my siblings, airport security lines, and the beautiful old buildings. I think I miss everything about the trip, good and bad.

I am going to write all about it for the newspaper.

I have a million ideas and can't wait to begin!

The AMAZING DAYS of
ABBY HAYES ®

by Anne Mazer

Read them all!

SCHOLASTIC